WITHDRAWN

D1180753

Published by Collins Educational
An imprint of HarperCollins*Publishers* Ltd
77-85 Fulham Palace Road
London W6 8JB

The HarperCollins website address is:
www.**fire**and**water**.com

First published by Hamlyn Publishing 1985
Second edition published by Thomas Nelson and Sons Ltd 1989
This edition published 1996 by Collins Educational
Reprinted 1999

ISBN 0 00 303261 2

British Library Cataloguing in Publication Data
A catalogue record for this book is available from the British Library.

Printed by Printing Express Ltd, Hong Kong

LETTERLAND HOME LEARNING
**HarperCollins publishes a wide range of Letterland early
learning books, video and audio tapes, puzzles and games.
For an information leaflet about Letterland or to order materials
call 0870 0100 441.**

Mayor Peter's Penguin Pals

Written by Stephanie Laslett
Illustrated by Maggie Downer

Collins

An imprint of HarperCollins*Publishers*

Letterland was having a heatwave, and everyone was hot and bothered. Poor Peter was trying to cool off in the park, without much success.

"My poor paws!" he moaned.
"This path is too hot to walk on."
Through the trees he could see clear, sparkling water.
"Perfect!" said Poor Peter. "The paddling pool will cool my paws!"

He hadn't been paddling for long when something pulled his tail.
"Ouch!" he cried. He turned round just in time to see a dark shape swim past him under the water.

Poor Peter was puzzled. "What was that?" he wondered. Just then a glossy, black head popped up above the water.

"Hello," it said. "My name is Polly Penguin. Would you like to play?" But before Poor Peter could answer he felt another pull on his tail.

"Ouch, ouch!" he cried. "I do beg your pardon," said the penguin. "That's my brother Paul. He's pretending that your tail is a fish. He would like to play too!"

"All right!" replied Poor Peter. "As long as there is no more tail-pulling."

After playing for a while Poor
Peter started to feel peckish.
"Would you like to share my
picnic?" he asked the penguins.
"Yes, please!" they replied.

So Poor Peter unpacked his picnic.
There were pieces of pizza, peanuts,
peaches and some fizzy pop.
"All my favourites," said Poor Peter.

But the penguins looked unhappy.
"Don't you like pizza?" asked Poor
Peter.
"No," they said, shaking their heads.
"But you probably like peanuts,"
said Poor Peter. They shook their
heads again.
"We only like fish!" they said together.

"We're hungry ... and we're hot," said the penguins. "We've had a lovely time in Letterland, but now we want to go home. It is nice and cold there — and there are lots of fish to eat."

"But where is home?" asked Poor Peter. The penguins looked puzzled. "We live at the Pole," they said. "Do you know how we can get back there?" "No," said Poor Peter. "But Munching Mike's map will tell us!"

Munching Mike showed them his map of the world. At once Polly pointed to the white part, right at the top. "The Pole!" she shouted excitedly.

Poor Peter looked closely at the map. The penguin was pointing to the North Pole.
"Well done," said Poor Peter.
"We will leave as soon as possible."
"But who will take us there?" pondered the penguins.

"Why not ask Jumping Jim?" suggested Munching Mike. "He can take you in his jet."

Jumping Jim was very happy to help. "A trip to the Pole? Great!" he said.

Soon Poor Peter and the penguins were flying high over the sea in Jim's powerful jet plane.

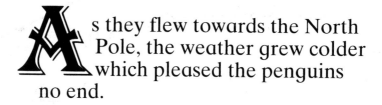

As they flew towards the North Pole, the weather grew colder which pleased the penguins no end.

"Nice and icy. Perfect!" they said.

Far below them huge icebergs floated in the sea. Soon they could see a big frozen icecap stretching out before them. The sun was gleaming and sparkling on the white snow.

"Here we are," called out Jumping Jim. "Please put your seats in the upright position, and fasten your seatbelts. We're ready to land."

"That was fun!" laughed the penguins as they jumped out of the jet. But Poor Peter was too busy shivering to speak. "It's freezing," he stuttered. "I'm perishing!"

"You're lucky," replied the penguins. "You can wrap your ears around your head to keep you warm." That made Poor Peter smile. Usually he found his ears too long and droopy. Now for once they were perfect!

"Is this the right place?" Poor Peter asked the penguins. "Yes," Polly replied happily. "It's cold and snowy and..."

Just then there was a loud growling noise behind them. "Grrrrr!" it went.

"Help!" cried the penguins as a huge, shaggy, white bear appeared. "That's not a penguin. What is it?"
"It's a p...p...p...polar bear," said Poor Peter. "But I will p...p...p...protect you," he added bravely.

"Who are you?" growled the bear. "And what sort of animals are you?"
"I'm P...P...P...Poor Peter," stuttered Peter. "And I'm a puppy."
"And we are Polly and Paul," said Polly. "We are penguins and we live here," she added proudly.

"Oh, no, you don't," said the polar bear. "I know everyone who lives here, and there are no penguins in this place."

Poor Polly and Paul were very upset. "Don't worry," said the polar bear (who was really very pleasant). "My friend the porpoise tells me that there is another Pole — way down at the other end of the Earth. It's called the South Pole, I think."

"SOUTH Pole!" shouted Polly. "That's where we live."

"Back to the plane," said Poor Peter.

It was a long way to the South Pole. They flew for hours and hours until far below the ground became white with snow.

"We're home!" cried Polly and Paul happily, for wherever they looked there were penguins, swimming, diving, even throwing snowballs. As they landed loud squawking noises filled the air. It was Polly and Paul's mum.

"My precious penguins!" she cried. "I am so pleased to see you both!"

Soon it was time for Poor Peter and Jumping Jim to leave.

"Thank you for your help," said the penguins.
"It was a pleasure!" replied Poor Peter and Jumping Jim.

A few weeks later, the postman brought Poor Peter a big postcard. On one side it said: "We had a lovely time in Letterland. Thank you for helping us to find our way home. From your pals, Polly and Paul."

"How wonderful," said Poor Peter happily. "I've never had a pen friend before and now I've got two — Polly and Paul, my penguin pen pals." And he sat down to write them a letter straight away.

THE END